DATE DUE		
NOV 5 '79		
JAN 16 '80		
NOV 14 '80		
DC 26 '84		
DE 09 '86		
OC 5 '90		
AR 16 '93		

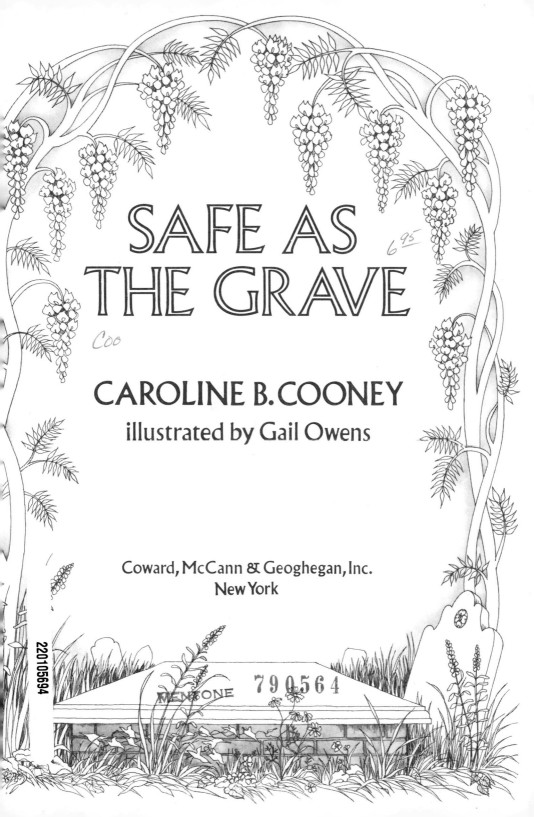

SAFE AS THE GRAVE

CAROLINE B. COONEY

illustrated by Gail Owens

Coward, McCann & Geoghegan, Inc.
New York

For Louisa Willerton and Sayre Elizabeth

Text copyright © 1979 by Caroline B. Cooney

Illustrations copyright © 1979 by Gail Owens

LIBRARY OF CONGRESS CATALOGING IN PUBLICATION DATA

Cooney, Caroline B.   Safe as the grave.

SUMMARY: A young girl inadvertently discovers clues
leading to a long-lost treasure.

[1. Buried treasure—Fiction]   I. Owens, Gail.   II. Title.
PZ7.C7834Saf   [Fic]   78-24412   ISBN 0-698-20479-4

Designed by Diane Zuromskis

Printed in the United States of America

Contents

1
The Graveyard Picnic

"Pretend we're hacking our way through the Amazon jungles," said Lynn, crouching to avoid a poison-tipped arrow.

Victoria jerked at a wisteria vine which refused to be ripped up. She mopped the sweat off her forehead and glared at her sister. "I don't have to pretend. This *is* a jungle. The mosquitoes are eating me alive."

"Pretend they're cannibals," said Lynn, "taking tiny bites. Waiting for the water to boil."

"Ugh," said Victoria. "You're more bother than the bugs, Lynn. Go away."

Lynn sighed. She and Victoria were twins, but they never understood each other. It seemed to Lynn if you had to be a twin, you at least ought to have something in common. She and Victoria were like breakfast cereals: Lynn snapped, crackled, and popped, but Victoria was oatmeal—solid and filling.

"If you pretend this is exciting," Lynn said, "then it won't be hard work. It'll be an adventure."

"This is our back yard. Full of weeds. I am not having an adventure."

My beautiful meadow? My dark, scary pine woods? How can she call them *our back yard?* thought Lynn. Carefully she stepped over the brush pile, in case it hid a pit full of spears.

"Stop daydreaming, Lynn," said her father, "and do your share."

Lynn began snipping with pruning shears at the tiny cottonwoods which had seeded themselves in the grass. Each autumn the Greers had to spend a day or two tearing out the weeds and brush which grew up in the family graveyard. The graveyard was out in the meadow, just barely in sight of the house. It had three lovely crape myrtle trees, blooming purple and maroon, and a hedge of privet. Around the privet was a low brick wall and over the gate was an iron trellis with a wisteria vine. The vine was huge and strong and tried every year to engulf the trees and pull over the gravestones.

Lynn was drenched with perspiration. Her father had seen some poison ivy and made everyone wear long sleeves, jeans, scarves, and work gloves. She had never been so hot in her whole life. But jungles are like that, she told herself. She stared along the wisteria vine to see if a python was about to drop on her.

"Lynn," said her father, "work, please."

"Why?"

"Because we are pressed for time."

"Why?"

"Because the weather reports say we're in for rain, rain, and more rain, and if you think this is a rotten chore in the sunshine, wait until you try it in the rain."

"Good point," said Lynn. She stuffed weeds into a huge black plastic bag and tried to fasten the top with a twisty wire. She succeeded in fastening her glove to the bag.

"I hate these gloves," she told Victoria. "They get in my way."

Victoria shrugged. Her gloves fit perfectly. "Pretend the cannibals are holding you prisoner," she said.

Lynn decided not to wear the gloves anymore. She hadn't seen any poison ivy. She never caught it anyway. Daddy was the only one who got rashes.

"Let's take a break," said their mother. "Anyone for lunch?"

"Yes!" shouted Lynn and Victoria. (Food was the only thing they agreed on.)

Mrs. Greer spread a red-and-white checked cloth over the tabletop grave at the edge of the burying ground. All the stones but this one were upright, with chipped inscriptions. They were graves of Greers back to the early 1800s. The thick, smooth slab of stone resting on its little foundation of crumbling bricks made a perfect table.

"Some people," said Victoria, "might think it was odd to have a picnic on top of a grave."

"It *is* odd," said Lynn. "That's why it's such fun."

Their mother spread out sandwiches, pickles, a thermos of iced tea, a bag of potato chips, and paper napkins. Lynn stuffed her gloves under a convenient pile of vines, vowing not to put them on again, and took a chicken salad sandwich.

"Look at those clouds," said their father. "It's a good thing we're almost done. Do you know they're expecting a hurricane to hit the coast in a few days? We'll catch the edges of it, I'm sure."

Lynn thought it would be much more interesting to catch

all of the hurricane. "How neat," she said. "Maybe we'll float away."

"Hush and eat your sandwich," scolded her mother. "It would *not* be neat."

Lynn squashed her sandwich until the chicken salad oozed out the edges and fell into her mouth. Then she licked her fingers. I'd better not let Mother see me working without gloves, she thought. Mother would moan and groan about Rules, and When Will You Ever Be Good Like Victoria? and When Will You Ever Do As You Are Told?

Lynn took another chicken salad sandwich. I don't mind being good, she thought, but I sure hate doing what I'm told.

"Who was Cornelia, anyway?" asked Victoria, reading the gravestone.

"Cornelia?" repeated their father.

"After all, we're eating off her gravestone," said Victoria. "It would be nice to know who she was."

"Oh. That Cornelia. No one knows who she was."

"Don't be silly, Daddy," said Lynn. "This is our burying ground. Everybody here is related to us." She moved the red-and-white cloth to see the inscription.

Cornelia 12 July 1863

"That day," said Mrs. Greer, "was the day before the only skirmish that occurred in our town during the Civil War. There weren't many battles in this part of North Carolina. The fighting was in Virginia. But sometimes the Union soldiers came through on raids. On July 13, 1863, they burned the cotton mills, the railroad bridge, and the telegraph office."

9

Lynn's jungle disappeared. Beyond the privet hedge she could hear the distant rhythm of marching feet. Against the horizon she saw flames licking the trees and homes of her town.

"But what about Cornelia?" said Victoria.

"No one knows. Isn't that sad?" said Mrs. Greer. "The day before the raid must have been a dreadful muddle. People running away and hiding things and lying low. Maybe Cornelia was some wanderer who lost her home and landed here. Maybe she was an old woman of eighty-six, or a newborn baby."

"Maybe she was eleven, like me," said Lynn. "Shot down by a Union soldier as she fled before the flames."

"Nope. Nobody got hurt in that raid," said her father. "No houses were burned, no people shot. The soldiers were just trying to destroy the railroad that was supplying General Lee's armies in Virginia. As for Cornelia, the only thing we can be sure of is that she wasn't a baby. This stone is five feet long. They wouldn't have used a huge stone like this on a tiny baby."

Thoughtfully, Lynn ate her sandwich crust. So this was the grave of a stranger. Had Cornelia been a stranger when she died here? Or a friend of the family, mourned in death?

"Who was living on our land then?" Victoria wanted to know.

"Let me think. That would have been your great-great-great-grandmother, Eppie Greer."

"Eppie?" said Victoria, shuddering. "I don't care for the name Victoria. But now I see it could be worse."

"Think of the first day of school," agreed Lynn. "Everyone laughing insanely and yelling, *Eppie! Eppie!*"

"Nobody laughed at Eppie Greer," said their father. "She

was quite a woman. Born in England, educated like her brothers, ran off with an American planter her parents disapproved of, came here to raise six sons and hold the farm together during a civil war."

Lynn hoped her grown-up years would be as exciting as Eppie's. But what a dreadful name. How could Lynn daydream that she was someone named Eppie?

"Her real name," said Mrs. Greer, "was Euphemia. See her grave over there?"

Euphemia Anne Greer
beloved wife of Charles
b. 12 April 1822
d. 28 September 1863

While everyone else was reading the inscription, Lynn finished the iced tea. "Didn't you bring any dessert, Mother?" she said. "Eppie didn't live much longer than Cornelia, did she?"

"No dessert. And she died of something they called river flux. Furthermore, I liked the story of Eppie so much that I wanted to name you for her, Lynn. Euphemia Lynn Greer. I thought we'd call you Yoofie for short."

Lynn choked on her tea.

Victoria laughed. "Yoofie," she said. "I like that." She said "Yoofie" about twenty times, like someone calling ducks to give them bread crusts.

"I'll strangle you with my wisteria vine if you don't stop calling me Yoofie!" shrieked Lynn.

But from the way Victoria promised never to call her Yoofie again, Lynn knew perfectly well that Victoria intended to call her that every chance she got.

11

"Back to work," said Mr. Greer, "before those clouds empty on us." He took the big shovel and went around the brick wall to dig up a sapling.

Lynn pulled out weeds and vines around Euphemia's grave. Eppie . . . she thought. With her bare finger, she traced the letters in the stone. What was the war like? Who was Cornelia? Was she a friend of yours, Eppie? Was she eleven, like me? Why did she get such a special grave?

2
But <u>Somebody</u> Died!

The rain came down ferociously, just the way Lynn thought it must rain in the tropics. Way down by the Tar River she could see trees bending in the fierce wind, see the surface of the water pockmarked where rain pelted it.

"I have a million errands to run," said Mother. "And a meeting at St. Stephen's."

"Let's stay home, Victoria," said Lynn. "And play Monopoly. Or watch TV."

"No," said Victoria. "I want to go on errands. I like errands."

"You can stay home alone, Lynnie," said Mother.

"I hate staying home alone. There's no one to play with. This is a teachers' holiday and there's no school. We're supposed to be having fun, not going on errands."

"Make up your mind," said Mother. "I'm leaving."

"What will we do during that old meeting at church?" said Lynn.

"The meeting will be brief," said Mother.

Lynn made a face. "Are you sure you know what brief means?" she muttered.

"Lynn, be courteous," said her mother. "Get on your raincoat, please, and run for the car."

Lynn stomped to the coat closet. Some day off from school this was turning out to be. Yesterday weeding, today errands. It made her so mad that she couldn't find the armholes of her raincoat.

"Even first graders can get their own coats on, Yoofie," said Victoria, sliding deftly into hers.

"Do you want me to stuff my scarf down your throat?" demanded Lynn.

"Mother!" shrieked Victoria. "Lynn's trying to hurt me!"

So Lynn had to sit in the back seat by herself and couldn't go in when Mother stopped at Aunt Mary's. Aunt Mary always said, "Sugar, have a chocolate-covered mint."

Victoria sauntered back to the car noisily sucking on a mint. She hadn't even brought one for Lynn.

After the dry cleaners and the post office and the drugstore and the bank, Mother said, "St. Stephen's next. You two can sit quietly in the church parlor till I'm done."

"*I* can sit quietly in the parlor," said Victoria. "Lynn never sits quietly anywhere."

"I know Lynn will try to be good," said Mother optimistically.

It was so boring always having to try to be good. Lynn had heard on a television talk show that you should be natural. "Be yourself," stressed the psychologist. Victoria was naturally good. Lynn was naturally not.

"Won't you, Lynn?" said Mother.

"Won't I what?"

"Try to be good?"

"Of course," said Lynn. Under her breath she added, "But not very hard."

14

All of Mother's kissy friends were there, in their elegant pants suits and gold necklaces and beauty-parlor hair. Victoria, who looked charming although she'd run through the rain more than Lynn had, offered her cheek for the kisses. Lynn, who was grubby and didn't have on matching socks, sat on the bottom hall step in her grumpiest slouch so no one could bend over and grab her cheek.

Off went the women into their meeting room, laughing and chattering about totally uninteresting things. Then the door shut.

"Good," said Lynn. "What shall we do now, Victoria?"

"We shall sit quietly in the church parlor," said her sister primly.

"There is nothing in the parlor but dusty books and an Oriental rug. It's boring."

"It's what we're supposed to do," said Victoria, and she pranced down the hall.

"Phooey," said Lynn.

It was a terrible afternoon. Lynn felt that if the day was terrible, the least she could do was to be terrible, too. That way things would be even.

She hopped up the stairs on one leg, having broken the other in the plane crash, to see if there was any survival food hidden in the playroom cupboards.

There wasn't.

She slid down the banister, Bionic Woman to the rescue, but she had grown over the summer. She didn't fit on the banister anymore.

She wandered into the hall where everyone gathered for coffee before services on Sundays. Lying on the floor was a Raggedy Ann some child had dropped. Lynn picked it up. She thought, It would be *good* to put this away . . . so I won't.

15

The only place left to explore was the sanctuary with its stained glass and dark crimson velvets and glittery candlesticks. Very little light filtered through the windows. Rain and thunder sounded dimly outside. Spooky, thought Lynn pleasurably.

Furthermore, the Raggedy Ann was just the right size to hang on the altar cross. Lynn twisted its arms around the gold cross and stepped back to admire her handiwork.

"Lynn," said Father Arden, "I cannot say I care for that."

"Oh, hi, Father," said Lynn weakly.

"Kindly remove Raggedy Ann."

Lynn obeyed.

"Come with me to my office," said Father Arden. "You and I need to have a little chat."

He doesn't mean a little chat, he means a big scolding, thought Lynn, almost sick to her stomach. He'll tell Mother. He'll tell Victoria. He'll tell Daddy.

"I'm sorry, Father."

Father Arden kept marching toward his office.

Lynn thought hard. "Father," she said, "could you help me with something? I need to know who Cornelia was. Cornelia—the one whose grave is on our family plot. Is she in the church records? She died July 12, 1863. Would you look her up for me? Please?"

Father Arden looked less threatening. "Surely, Lynn. It's nice to see you interested in history."

The old church records were in a fireproof safe in the closet of his office. The book he reached for was a leather-bound volume with very thick vanilla pages and spidery brown script on fat black lines.

"The Church of St. Stephen was founded in 1818," said

17

Father Arden. "Your ancestors were very active in it. Although I do not recall that anyone other than you ever hung a rag doll on the cross." He gave Lynn half a glare through his bifocals. Lynn looked back at him, half sorry.

"Your great-great-great-grandmother Eppie Greer was the one who embroidered the original altar cloths, you know. We still have all those. She did beautiful work. Most elegant."

Embroidering altar cloths seemed quite a step down for the English girl who'd run away from home to marry an American planter and run a pioneer farm, thought Lynn. If Euphemia had ambushed some Union soldiers, now *that* would be exciting.

"During the Civil War," Father Arden went on, "Euphemia's cousin from England, Father Sayre, was rector here. That was when we lost the beautiful jeweled cross that he brought with him from England. Apparently the Yankees took it."

"What jeweled cross?" cried Lynn. "I've never heard that story."

But Father Arden was gently leafing through the pages of the church records, looking for Cornelia. "April 1863," he announced. "Two men lost with Lee's armies in Virginia. May 1863. One baby died at age two weeks. One slave died of river flux. One woman died in childbirth. June 1863, no deaths recorded. July 1863, no deaths recorded."

"No deaths," repeated Lynn. "Does that mean that Cornelia was not an Episcopalian? That her death is recorded somewhere else?"

"The only other church here at that time was the West Brook Baptist Church, and they lost all their records in a fire in the 1920s. But if Cornelia was buried in your family graveyard, the Episcopal priest would have presided. Especially since he was Eppie's cousin."

"Maybe he forgot to record it."

"No. It says right here in his handwriting, 'No Deaths.' "

Lynn did not know what to make of that, but she had succeeded in taking Father's mind off the Raggedy Ann, so she didn't mind. "Now tell me about the jeweled cross, okay?"

"No, it's not okay. Here is a book to read instead."

It was fat and dusty. *St. Stephen's and Its Parish: A History from 1818 Until the Close of the War Between the States.* Two hundred and eighty-four pages.

Lynn did not believe anyone was that interested in the history of St. Stephen's.

"As much of the story as we know is in those pages," Father Arden told her. "This will be your penance for hanging a Raggedy Ann on the cross. Read up on the history of the church your great-great-great-grandmother loved so much."

"Wonderful," said Lynn glumly.

Father Arden's eyes behind the bifocals became severe. "Be pleasant about it or I'll have to have a talk with your parents."

Lynn rolled her eyes. "Wonderful!" she cried falsely. "I can't wait. Won't it be fun."

Victoria came in. "What will be fun?" she said. "I want to do it, too. Lynn, you have to share. Let me do it, too."

"Sure," said Lynn, cheerful at last. "You get to read the first hundred pages of this book!"

3
Lynn Is Rained Out

"Poison ivy," said her mother. "It was all over Eppie's grave. We told you to leave your work gloves on, but no, you had to take them off."

Lynn tried not to cry. The rash was between each finger, on the palms of her hands, edging up her wrists. It itched evilly. She could not think about anything except how much it itched.

"Spread out your fingers till none of them touch," said her mother. "The calamine lotion will take away some of the itch." Lynn spread her hands over a towel so her mother could pour the thick liquid over them. While it was wet she felt better. Sloshy, but better.

"I propped a book open for you," said Victoria, "on your bed. But you can't turn pages or you'll get pink gook on them."

Lynn ignored her. It was just like Victoria not to get poison ivy. It was even more like Victoria to give Lynn a book and tell her not to turn any pages.

She stared at her hands as the calamine dried. Now she had fat pink crusts on her skin, like some ghastly tropical disease illustrated in her encyclopedia. When she crooked a finger, the crust split and the rash showed through.

"Too bad," said her mother. "Field days at school and you have to miss them."

"Both days?" moaned Lynn, thinking of sack races and treasure hunts and candy-bar prizes.

"Until the rash goes away. Now. I'm going to drive Victoria to school, since she missed the bus, and then I have some shopping to do. I'll be back by lunch."

"I'll be bored if I have to stay all by myself all morning," Lynn grumbled.

"It will teach you a lesson," said her mother.

Everyone wanted Lynn to learn a lesson. She made a face. "But what'll I do all morning? I can't touch anything."

Victoria laughed at her. "Pretend your friends the cannibals tied you up, Yoofie."

"Drop dead," said Lynn. Then she had a better idea. She took a swipe at Victoria's face with her rashy hands.

"Lynn!" said her mother furiously. "Behave yourself. Victoria, stop starting things."

Morosely, Lynn watched them drive away. A whole morning with nothing to do but feel herself itch. And not scratch.

She looped the towel around her hands, went into the den, and turned on the TV with her teeth. It kept calamine lotion off the dial, but made dents in her lips.

"News," she said disgustedly. "Who cares about the news?"

She lay on her back and turned the channel dial with her toes. Her left foot was better at turning. Cartoons. News. Quiz. Quiz. Kid show. Quiz.

She stayed on the quiz instead of going back to the

cartoons because her toes hurt. A woman was guessing the prices of soap powder and handbags. The woman leaped up and down as if several tiny dogs were nipping at her heels. Lynn decided to do everything the contestants did. For the next half hour she bounced and squealed and hugged the emcee.

"My hands itch," Lynn told the emcee.

He smiled at her.

"They itch so bad I'm going to scream in one minute." She wondered if she could scream so loudly that motorists driving past would think she was being murdered. That would make the morning more interesting.

But when Lynn opened the front door to scream, she got a mouthful of rain. "Well," she said to no one, "at least Victoria has to have field day in the gym."

Across the farm she could see the Tar River edging over its banks. Patches of standing water dotted the red clay fields where stubs of harvested tobacco plants were drowning. With all the racket the rain was making, no one was going to hear her scream.

"AAAAAHHHHH!" she screamed. "MY POOR HANDS! AAAAAHHHHH!"

Her hands did not itch any less and now her hair was wet.

"Some ancestor you are, Euphemia Greer!" yelled Lynn. "Poison ivying your own great-great-great-granddaughter."

She went into her bedroom to find the book Victoria had propped open. She had expected to see the history of St. Stephen's turned to something exciting like the index, but this book was called *Tiny Tales of Ancient Rome for Good Little Boys and Girls.*

"Ugh," said Lynn. "Where did Victoria find this awful old

thing? I bet she looked all day yesterday to find the worst possible book in the whole attic."

Lynn read the open page anyway. It was about a man named Horatius who lived in ancient Rome. He was the only one in the Roman army brave enough to guard a bridge against the Etruscan army. The Romans and the Etruscans were very impressed with Horatius, but Lynn thought he was crazy. "A man could get hurt that way, Horatius," she told him.

She wanted to turn the page to find out what happened to Horatius, but her fingers were stuck together with calamine glue. After considering the problem for a while, Lynn turned the page with her tongue. It tasted dusty.

The phone rang.

"Don't worry, Horatius, I'll be back. Hold that bridge." She ran downstairs. There seemed to be no way to answer the phone with her toes, so she used her fingers. Pink crust crumbled all over the telephone table. "Hello?"

"It's Mother. Are you doing all right?"

"Yes."

"The doctor says to bring you in and he'll give you a shot, so I'm—"

"A shot! No, no, I'm fine. It hardly itches at all," babbled Lynn.

"—coming home in ten minutes to get you."

Click.

Lynn went sadly upstairs and found out that brave Horatius had saved everybody, including himself, and had not even gotten hurt. "It's easy for you to be brave, Horatius," she told him. "They didn't have shots in those days. And I bet you'd have deserted that old bridge if you'd

24

had poison ivy. You would have been too busy itching and scratching to hold onto your javelin."

The next chapter looked thrilling. "A Roman Matron Has a Busy Day, Weaving, Cooking, and Fetching Water." "Ugh," said Lynn. That made even a history of St. Stephen's look good.

"I know what happened to Cornelia," she told her mother darkly. "She read a book about ancient Rome that was so boring she fell asleep in the poison ivy patch and died of itchy rashes."

"As long as you've learned your lesson," said her mother.

"I've learned to stand on the bridge no matter how dangerous it looks."

"What bridge?" said Mrs. Greer. "The lesson is, stay out of poison ivy."

"Oh, that lesson. You know, Mother, as long as I have poison ivy anyway, I think I will spend the night on Cornelia's grave and see if she will come and tell me who she was."

But it rained all night and all the next day and all day Saturday, so that reaching Cornelia's grave would have been like wading through a swamp. Lynn watched her blisters dry up while her parents complained about the rain. It should have rained in the spring when they needed it. It should have spread itself out in lots of gentle showers instead of one unremitting deluge. It should be in another state where *they* needed rain.

"If it rains again tomorrow," said her father, "I may have to build an ark."

"If it rains again tomorrow," said her mother, "I shall go berserk."

Lynn dragged herself through several chapters of St. Stephen's history and switched to *Tiny Tales* when she decided that she knew more about the education of nineteenth-century Episcopal rectors than any human being needed to know. "Well, look at this, Mother," she said suddenly. "Right here on the flyleaf of *Tiny Tales*, it says: *Euphemia Anne, her book*. And it was published in England. Eppie liked this book enough to bring it with her when she ran off with great-great-great-grandfather Greer."

"Poor Euphemia," said Mother. "If that was the best story she had, reading must have been dreary business in those days."

"And here's something else!" cried Lynn.

"Keep calm, Yoofie," said Victoria. "There is nothing in that book to make anyone shout with glee."

Lynn ignored her. She was just trying to make the best of the millionth rainy day in a row. "On the chapter page, you know, where they list all the chapters, Euphemia has circled one chapter and starred it and written *a tale to cherish*."

"I bet it's the one on fetching water," said Victoria.

Before Lynn had a chance to whack Victoria with Euphemia's book, their father rushed into the room, yelling, "Quick! Everybody outside."

"Why?" said Lynn, not moving. "Is the house on fire?"

"Run!" he yelled. "It's stopped raining. No time to waste. Got to get it done right this minute."

Something exciting at last, thought Lynn, and she set

Eppie's book down and forgot all about the chapter her great-great-great-grandmother had circled and starred.

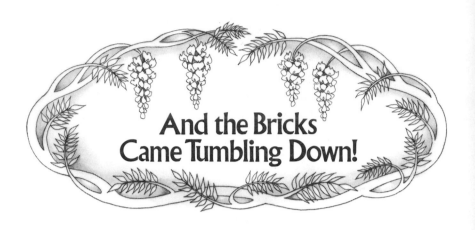

And the Bricks Came Tumbling Down!

They rushed across the muddy yard to the pickup truck. "Why are we running, Daddy?" panted Lynn.

"Because I expect the storm to start up again any minute, and with the high winds they're predicting for tonight, we have to get this job done."

"Job!" cried Lynn. "Do you mean to tell me that we are racing through the mud in order to *work*?"

"Right."

Lynn could see no reason to hurry if all they were going to do was work. She slowed down, which made her sneakers skid in the mud. *Splat!* Down she went into the soaking grass, getting red clay mud in her shoes and down her socks. It squooshed like the calamine lotion. "I'm always icky," she said ruefully.

"It suits you," agreed Victoria, walking sedately around the edges of puddles.

"Twins," said Lynn, reaching for her sister's ankle, "should match." She jerked hard. With a shriek and a splash, Victoria landed rear end first in a rut in the driveway.

"Lynn," said her mother furiously, "if you do one more thing to anger me I shall not let you go to Aunt Mary's birthday party tonight. Do you understand?"

Lynn sighed. Aunt Mary always made her own four-layer cake and pecan pie and peanut brittle because no one else baked as well as she did and Aunt Mary wanted *her* birthday to taste splendid. No one wanted to miss Aunt Mary's birthday party.

"Stop drawing in the mud with your sneaker, Lynn, and get in the truck and answer me," said her mother. "Are you going to be decent?"

"Yes, Mother." Actually Lynn felt she was much more decent than Victoria, but it seemed wise to be polite with a threat like missing Aunt Mary's party hanging over her head. "So what's the job, Daddy?" She slammed the door and all four of them sat scrunched in the front.

"We're pulling down the chimney at the old home place," said her father.

The old home place was down the lane, closer to the Tar River than the house they lived in now. Years ago the old home place had burned down and now only one chimney and the foundations were left. The chimney had a definite list to the west. Lynn loved it there, all alone and abandoned and mysterious in the fields by the river.

"You see," said Mother, "I put in all those blueberry bushes right next to it, and if these high winds come up, I kind of think the chimney will topple and I don't want my blueberry bushes flattened. So we'll pull it down now and make it fall in the other direction."

"Pull it down? Will we be safe?" said Victoria anxiously.

"Safe as the grave," her father answered cheerfully.

29

Lynn shivered. "What does that mean?"

"Very few things can happen to you after you're buried," said her father.

Lynn had to agree with that. "I see," she said. "Did Euphemia live in the old home place?"

"Sure did."

"Maybe she hid a love letter in the bricks," said Lynn, who had decided that with a handicap like the name Euphemia, Eppie had probably made up for it by leading a very romantic and exciting life.

"Not likely," said Mother unromantically. "And another reason the chimney bothers me is that it might fall and hit somebody."

"Only somebody dumb enough to be wandering in the fields during a windstorm," said Lynn, "like Victoria."

"You're the only dummy who would do that," said Victoria.

"Girls!" said their mother.

The twins made horrid faces at each other. Lynn's faces were much more revolting than Victoria's, who even stuck out her tongue neatly.

"I can't stand it," said their mother. "Eleven years old and they haven't improved."

"Remember when they were born and we thought what sweet companions they would be for each other?" said their father.

"My, you were innocent," Lynn told him.

Her mother laughed. "Now, my innocent daughters, allow me to tell you what we're going to do with the bricks from the chimney."

"What?" Lynn could feel a chore approaching.

"We are going to load them in the pickup, take them home, chip off the mortar, and build ourselves a patio."

"We are?" said Victoria faintly.

"We are," repeated their mother.

Mr. Greer stopped the truck about twenty feet from the chimney. He looped one end of a heavy rope around the chimney while Lynn tied the other end to the trailer hitch. "Good knot," complimented her father. Lynn beamed.

"James, I think we're too close. The chimney is going to hit the truck when it falls," said Mother nervously. "Somebody's going to get hurt."

"Emily, would I purposely use a rope that's too short?"

"Only if you wanted to get rid of Lynn," said Victoria.

"I'm going to feed you a brick for supper," Lynn told her sister.

"QUIET!" said their father. "And get in the truck."

But Lynn felt she could see better from outside the truck. "Okay, but move way, way over," said her father.

Lynn bounced through the tall wet weeds. She was so messy, nothing mattered now anyway.

Mr. Greer started the engine. Slowly he drove forward until the rope was taut and the pickup was straining.

"Daddy!" yelled Lynn. "Stop! There's nothing under your wheels but mud. You're going to get caught."

"I know what I'm doing, Lynn," said her father.

"But, Daddy—"

"But, Lynn," he yelled, "but me no buts!"

Lynn glared at him. Huffily she sat down on a rock, but it turned out to be a blueberry bush and she sank to the ground in a shower of wet leaves.

"Oh, ugh," said Lynn, very glad that Victoria had been looking the other way.

The truck pulled.

The chimney didn't move.

And the wheels began to spin in the mud.

"I told you so!" screamed Lynn. "Now you're stuck. I told you so."

Her father was mumbling as he got out of the truck to stare at the ruts he'd just dug himself into.

"James," said Mrs. Greer, "don't say things like that in front of the children."

Lynn immediately came close enough to hear what colorful words her father was spilling forth. "I told you so," she told him.

"And I told you," said her mother tensely, "that one more infuriating remark from you and you'd miss Aunt Mary's birthday party. So that's that. No party for you tonight."

Lynn glared at her mother. She glared at her father. She glared at Victoria, who sweetly smiled back. Victoria would get pecan pie and homemade peanut brittle and all the four-layer cake she could eat.

Lynn whirled and ran through the blueberry bushes and the weeds and the fields until she came to the graveyard, where she flopped down on Cornelia's stone. "Life is not fair, you guys," she told Cornelia and Euphemia. "Here I am being *right* and *I* have to miss the party."

And she found herself sliding off the stone right into the mud again.

Cornelia's grave was no longer horizontal. The huge flat stone was slanted like a sliding board. The ground had become so wet and so soft that the lower course of bricks

which held up the tabletop had sunk into the ground like Daddy's tires. There was no mortar and, where the bricks had shifted, there were gaping holes. If she'd had a flashlight, Lynn could have looked in on Cornelia's bones.

"Even I wouldn't do that, Cornelia," said Lynn. "In spite of what my mother thinks, I am a decent person. I do not allow myself to spy on skeletons."

But all the same, she wondered if the flashlight had new batteries in it or not.

5
Safe as the Grave

When the rain began again, Lynn reluctantly went home. The pickup truck, filled with chunks of chimney, was parked by the kitchen door. Lynn started to go in but her mother let out a yell. "Don't you bring mud into my clean house! Look at yourself."

Lynn looked. She was slimy with red clay. Her shoes and blue jeans and shirt were clinging wet. Her hair hung in matted snarls, and her poison ivy blisters had become bumps of mud.

"I'm going to strip you and spray you clean with the hose before you set foot in my kitchen, Elizabeth Lynn Greer," said her mother.

"Oh, good. I've never streaked before," said Lynn cheerfully. She flung off her clothes and danced naked under the spray. It really was a lot of fun, even if it was rather chilly. Usually September was hot, but the rainy weather had cooled the air.

"Ma," Lynn asked, "what do you know about the missing cross from St. Stephen's?"

"Very little. It was supposed to have been a magnificent

work of art, encrusted with precious gems. But I've never believed that. It was probably gold-plated with some cut glass sprinkled on it. When it got lost during the war, somebody made up a legend about it."

"You really know how to ruin a story," said Lynn disgustedly. "Don't you even think the Yankees took it?"

"No. I think the Yankees had better things to do than wander around country chapels looking for gold. They were here only a few hours, you know, and I expect they were fairly busy, what with setting fire to the cotton mills and the railroad bridge."

"But maybe they came back at night on a second raid and stole the cross then."

"The whole town certainly expected that. The people lived in fear for several years. They stashed their silver and precious things in odd corners just in case the Yankees did return and start to plunder. But it never happened."

"Maybe," cried Lynn, thinking of buried treasure and gold doubloons, "somebody hid the cross for safekeeping and then it was never found."

"For pity's sakes, Lynn. If somebody hid the cross, they'd bring it back to the church when the war was over. I expect it just got lost in the shuffle."

Lynn sighed.

"But," said her mother, "I hereby give you my permission to find the cross. I wouldn't object to a ransom in gold and precious gems."

"Okay, Ma," said Lynn. "I'm off on my treasure hunt." She giggled.

Her mother ruffled Lynn's wet hair. "Go get some clothes on, baby."

"Party clothes?" said Lynn, hoping.

"Bathrobe. I'll heat a can of ravioli for you. Sorry, but I stick to what I say. It's your own fault."

When they had all gone (Victoria prancing about in her fluffy yellow dress, chattering about a second helping of pie), Lynn forced herself to pick up the history of St. Stephen's and read up to the part where the raid took place.

It was very boring.

> It was at this time that fears in the village over possible raids by Union soldiers reached fever pitch. Like squirrels, the townspeople and planters buried everything they thought would be of value to a plundering soldier. And like squirrels, they often forgot where they had done their burying.

How about that! thought Lynn. Maybe I should dig around the old home place, like an archaeologist, and see what I come up with.

A few pages further on she found mention of Eppie.

> When news came that the Yankees might indeed exert their military strength in a great effort to destroy the exceedingly important bridge of the Richmond/Weldon railroad that supplied General Lee's armies, Euphemia Anne Greer became concerned that the fame of the St. Stephen cross might bring Union soldiers into the very sanctuary which she and her cousin, the Rector Sayre, had labored in such love to make a beautiful home for Our Lord.

That, thought Lynn, must be the world's longest sentence.

Mrs. Greer entrusted the safekeeping of the church linens and vestments to several of her neighbors. The alms basins, which were of gold and had been brought from England by Father Sayre, were buried near the vicarage and not retrieved until 1866. But the cross vanished. This cross, which stood 19 inches high on a 3-tiered base of gold, was adorned with sapphires and other gems of great worth. It was widely assumed that the Yankees succeeded in stealing it. The only other known damage wrought by the Yankees was the burning of a wagon train of 800 bales of cotton, which train they surprised on their return journey to Wilmington. This harvest had been grown by . . .

Lynn could not believe that a young woman who ran away from England in the face of her parents' wrath to marry an American planter, raise six sons, and keep a farm while her husband fought with General Lee would have allowed that cross to be stolen. If she had been worried about her altar embroidery, she certainly would have spared a thought for that cross.

Lynn read on, her eyes skimming rapidly, hoping for a clue. But there was only one more paragraph about the Greers.

Because the only stonemason had been with Lee in Richmond, no headstones were carved until 1868, when Father Sayre had the wooden name markers replaced. At the church's expense the unknown grave in the Greer burying ground was carved with the information Euphemia Greer had painted on a temporary wooden marker:

38

Lynn tried to imagine Cornelia's burial in the little family plot. She could see the Greer slaves gathered round the canvas-wrapped body of the unknown Cornelia, prepared for her eternal rest by Euphemia Greer. Had they wept for Cornelia? Had her great-great-great-grandmother said a quiet prayer as the slaves hoisted the heavy slab and shut Cornelia in the dark forever?

Lynn stared out the window at the burying ground across the fields. The rain came down in torrents. Clouds of black and purple rolled overhead. The old crape myrtle trees bent under the force of the wind. Beyond them the Tar River had escaped its banks. It crawled over the flat red clay, lapping at the grass and weeds.

"Okay, Euphemia, confess," said Lynn. "Where'd you put the cross?"

She wanted to find the cross and she wanted to find it RIGHT NOW. But it was night, and it was raining. Besides, she had not the slightest idea of where Euphemia might have buried it.

Probably near the old home place, where she could keep an eye on it.

But poor Eppie had died of river flux only a few months later. Yankees were still wandering all over the place and it wasn't safe to bring the cross out of hiding. Probably no one but Eppie had known the spot.

"That's it," whispered Lynn excitedly. "Eppie died without telling anybody where the treasure was. She was only forty-one, so she didn't expect to be dying. Why should she tell anyone? They might gossip and spread the secret and soon Yankee ears would know.

"I'm listening, Euphemia," Lynn whispered to her great-great-great-grandmother. "You can tell me."

But there was only the sound of the storm outside.

She watched television for a while, thinking about the four-layer cake and the sweet crunchy peanut brittle Victoria was having.

They kept interrupting the program with bulletins about flood dangers. Rivers were rising. Some streets without storm drains were completely flooded. Yards in low spots were knee deep in standing water. A car had been overturned in a parking lot when a creek rushed over its banks.

Lynn wished she lived downtown where exciting things like that happened.

There was nothing exciting here. No one to talk to, nothing good (like four-layer cake) to eat. The only thing left to read was Euphemia's *a tale to cherish*. Lynn decided to give that a chance.

She turned to the page Eppie had starred and circled. It said, "The Tale of a Very Good Mother."

It was about a mother in ancient Rome named Cornelia who had several children. Someone asked Cornelia why she didn't wear more jewelry to parties. Cornelia beamed a motherly smile. She placed her arms around her children's shoulders. "These," she said lovingly, "are my jewels."

"Oh, ick," said Lynn. "Super ick."

In her great-great-great-grandmother's handwriting, at the bottom of the last page of the chapter, it said, *A special joke, all for myself. Isn't this fun?*

The note was dated July 1, 1863. Two weeks before the Yankees raided, Lynn remembered.

She did not like the Roman story. Where is the fun in being dragged in front of grown-ups at a party to be hugged by your mother? She could just see that old Cornelia in her Roman robe, simpering over her beautiful children, and—

Cornelia?

A special joke, just for Euphemia? About Cornelia and her jewels?

What was it Daddy had said when they were pulling down the chimney? Something about "safe as the grave."

Now that, thought Lynn, is quite a joke.

"Eppie," she said, "if you would really do a thing like that, you are worthy of being my ancestor and I will name my daughter for you. Is it a deal?"

But there was only the sound of the storm outside.

Lynn flung on her raincoat and found the flashlight in her father's tool box. She tested it and it didn't work, which meant ten good minutes wasted scrounging through mechanical toys until she found a battery that worked.

She ran out of the house into the driving rain and the violent wind, across the muddy, uneven ground.

"Victoria was right. I am a dummy. Only a dummy would go out in a storm like this. But at least there isn't an old brick chimney to fall on me anymore."

In case Euphemia was wondering, she yelled, "I'm coming!".

She fell down three times in the mud just going through the yard. And even though it was her own field, where she had played all her life, she was not entirely sure where she was headed. It was so dark. So windy.

And so scary.

"I won't think about the scary part," Lynn told herself.

42

But when she climbed over the privet hedge and the low brick wall and fell into the graveyard, things got even scarier. Rain pounded her. She caught her foot on something and something else stroked her cheek. "Oh," moaned Lynn, cringing. But it was only a crape myrtle, split down the middle and lying across the stone.

Lynn felt around for Cornelia's slab. The rain fell in a shiny black river down its slanted top. Her flashlight picked out the letters of Cornelia's name.

Oh, but what if I'm wrong? she thought. What if there *is* a person under that gravestone and I reach in to get sapphires and I get bones? *What will I do if I pull out a leg?*

She shuddered and almost dropped the flashlight. But then she took a deep, steadying breath of air, crouched in the mud, and aimed her flash between the bricks.

The battery died.

She didn't have to pretend the scream now. It came all by itself, shattering the stillness.

And then lightning pierced the sky. A great streak of it, illuminating the farm and then vanishing.

Lightning! thought Lynn in horror. And I'm in the most dangerous place in the whole world to be during a lightning storm.

She flattened herself in the mud next to Cornelia's grave, trembling.

6
Grave Secret

When she had been lying in the mud for what felt like thirty-seven hours, the rain stopped. The clouds were whisked away by angry winds and sprinkles of stars appeared in the blackness. Lynn sat up, so soggy and muddy she needed to be wrung out. She had mud in her hair, all the way up her raincoat sleeves, and even in her ears.

"Be thankful," Lynn told herself. "The lightning chose to pass you by."

She peered over the graveyard hedge. Every light at home was on. Through the windows she could see her mother rushing from room to room, calling.

It was pretty easy to guess who she was looking for.

"I can't go home like this," groaned Lynn. "What will I say? That I've been taking a nap in the graveyard? During a lightning storm?"

They would put chains around her legs and buy a dog with long white fangs to guard her in case she ever lost her mind again. They would never, never, ever let her go to Aunt Mary's for peanut brittle and four-layer cake.

Full of dread, Lynn sat down on Cornelia's grave and promptly slid off into the mud again. She was eye level with the holes in the bricks, and once more she tried to look into the grave. Whatever the funeral had been for, whatever Eppie had wrapped in canvas and ordered the slaves to cover with the stone, was lying in wait for Lynn. Canvas rotted. The bones—or the jewels—would be bare in the mud.

But it was no use. Her flashlight was out, and the stars were too dim. She could see nothing.

A really brave eleven-year-old, Lynn thought, would just stick her hand in the hole and feel around. She'd close her hand over something long and thin and hard and pull it out. Then she'd scrape off the mud and feel to see if there were sapphire bumps . . . or bony joints.

Lynn decided that she was not a really brave eleven-year-old.

But then again, reaching inside a grave would be no harder than telling her mother and father she had gone outside to play during a lightning storm. And if she came home with the missing cross, they might forgive her.

Lynn tried not to think what they would do if she came home with a skeleton.

She screwed her eyes shut, took a deep breath, and stuck her hand between the bricks.

Mud. Slimy, awful mud.

She slithered her hand around.

More mud.

I've never done anything so icky, she thought. Cornelia, if you are really in here, I'm sorry.

Suddenly . . . something hard, and long, and heavy.

45

Lynn pulled. And pulled some more. She moved another brick to make the opening wider and out came whatever it was.

Very few bones, thought Lynn, have square edges.

With her raincoat sleeve, she wiped the mud off. Something smooth and hard glistened in the dark. In her hands she felt the beautiful bejeweled cross Father Sayre had brought from England so many years before.

"Euphemia," Lynn told her great-great-great-grandmother, "that was some hiding place!"

Of course, the best part of the whole thing was that the newspaper put her photograph on the very front page of the Sunday edition.

LOCAL GIRL FINDS MISSING CIVIL WAR CROSS!

Lynn thought she looked absolutely terrific with her arm loosely draped around the gleaming, newly polished cross.

Aunt Mary made her an *eight*-layer cake. All chocolate.

Mother said, "You were right, Lynn. No bits of shiny glass. These are really precious jewels. And you are one intelligent young woman to have discovered Cornelia's secret."

Her father just shook his head and laughed.

"Aren't you even going to punish me for going out at night like that, Daddy?" said Lynn, who knew perfectly well he wasn't going to punish her. He'd been too happy just finding her alive and muddy.

"I don't have to punish you," said her father. "You've punished yourself."

"I have?"

"Look at your hands."

Lynn looked down.

Victoria began to laugh. "Back to zero, Yoofie," she said.

"Oh, no!" cried Lynn. "I not only spent the night lying in the mud, I spent it lying in the rest of the poison ivy!"

Once more she had to sit with her fingers stiff and stretched till the calamine turned to pink crusts on her hands.

"You *still* don't get any cake," said Victoria. "If you touch it, you'll get pink gook in it."

"Calamine lotion," said Lynn, "does not stop a front-page heroine from enjoying her chocolate cake."

Lynn put her hands behind her and stuck her face right in the cake and ate it doggy style. Victoria ate from the opposite side of the cake, no hands, no forks, until their noses met in the middle and Victoria said, "Woof, woof."

"No," said Lynn, muddy with chocolate icing, "Yoofie, Yoofie."